This Book Belongs to:

_____

ISBN 978-1-338-57713-6

10 9 8 7 6 5 4 3   20 21 22 23 24

First printing 2020 • Book design by Betsy Peterschmidt

Printed in Jefferson City, MO, U.S.A. 40
Scholastic Inc., 557 Broadway, New York, NY 10012
Scholastic UK Ltd., Euston House, 24 Eversholt Street, London NW1 1DB

Clifford The BIG RED DOG®

WATCH ON prime video

The Story of Clifford

Scholastic Inc.

Clifford created by
Norman Bridwell

Written by
Meredith Rusu

Illustrated by
Jen Oxley and
Erica Kepler

On Birdwell Island, the sun is always shining, and there is always a new adventure on the horizon.

That's because Emily Elizabeth and Clifford the Big Red Dog live here.

And when you're friends with a dog like Clifford, all your adventures are BIG.

Emily Elizabeth and Clifford have been best friends
ever since he was a puppy.

Clifford used to be little.

But then he grew . . . and grew . . . and GREW.

Now Clifford and Emily Elizabeth spend every day laughing, pretending, and telling stories.

Clifford and Emily Elizabeth always have so much fun together.

That's because they are best friends.

One morning, Clifford was feeling extra playful.

"Let's have a parade, Emily Elizabeth!" he said.

"A parade?" Emily Elizabeth asked. "What are we celebrating?"

"It just feels like a parade sort of day," said Clifford.

Emily Elizabeth grinned. "That's a great idea!
It will be our very own Birdwell Island Parade."

THE BIG BIRDWELL ISLAND PARADE

Emily Elizabeth and Clifford got to work.

They blew up balloons and painted a banner.

Emily Elizabeth even helped Clifford make a parade-leader hat.

Just then, Emily Elizabeth's friend Sam stopped by. "Hi, guys! What are you doing?"

"We're having a parade!" Emily Elizabeth exclaimed.

"Can I join, too?" asked Sam.

"Woof!" said Clifford. That meant, "Of course!"

It was time for the parade to start.

Emily Elizabeth and Sam got into place. Clifford led the way.

"AH-WOOF! WOOF! WOOF-WOOF-WOOF!"

With happy smiles and Clifford's bark keeping the beat, off went the three-person parade!

The parade marched past the park.

Emily Elizabeth and Sam spotted their friends Jack and Pablo.

They were playing fetch with Clifford's doggy pals Bailey and Tucker.

"We're having a Birdwell Island Parade!" Emily Elizabeth shouted to them. "Come join us!"

"A parade?" Tucker barked to Clifford. "Oh boy, oh boy! You know I love parades!"

"We're in!" woofed Bailey.

Clifford led his friends past the docks and toward
Mrs. Clayton and the Birdwell Island Library Boat.

THE BIG
BIRDWELL ISLAND
PARADE

"How exciting!" Mrs. Clayton said when she saw them.
"You're having a Founder's Day Parade."

"It's not a Founder's Day Parade." Emily Elizabeth giggled.
"It's just for fun."

"But today is the day Birdwell Island was founded," Mrs. Clayton told them. "Your parade is right on time!"

Emily Elizabeth gasped. "Clifford, our Birdwell Island Parade just turned into a Birdwell Island *Birthday* Parade!"

The kids made a quick change to their banner.
Then they marched on.

They were ready to tell everyone they saw that
today was Birdwell Island's birthday!

When the parade reached the town square, Ms. Ellerby stopped traffic so they could cross.

Drivers waved and some even shouted, "Happy birthday, Birdwell Island!"

Soon, the friends arrived at Emily Elizabeth's parents' gift shop, the Sea Shell.

"Hi, honey!" Her mom and dad came over to greet them. "What's all this?"

"We're having a parade to celebrate Birdwell Island's birthday!" Emily Elizabeth explained. "Can we borrow an island flag?"

"Of course!" said Emily Elizabeth's dad. "One Birdwell Island flag coming right up."

With the flag in hand, Emily Elizabeth, Clifford, and their friends were ready to continue the fun.

But as soon as they got outside, they stopped. They stared. They couldn't believe their eyes.

A huge group of townspeople was outside holding their own balloons, banners, and confetti.

It looked like the whole island had gathered to meet them!

"We heard you're having a Birdwell Island Parade," Ms. Lee said.

"To celebrate the island's founding," Fisherman Charlie added.

"And we want to join!" a group of kids cheered.

Emily Elizabeth and Clifford grinned from ear to ear.

"Of course!" she cried. "A Birdwell Island Birthday Parade is even better when everyone on Birdwell Island joins in!"

And so, the parade marched on!

People hurried from every house, and shop owners scurried from every store.

Everyone was joining the parade!

Before long, the parade line stretched, way, *way* back.

But everyone was able to keep up.

After all, it's easy to follow along when the parade leader is as big as Clifford the Big Red Dog.

At the end of the parade, the whole island gathered in the town square.

Everyone danced and played. It was the perfect ending to the perfect parade!

Emily Elizabeth gave Clifford a great big hug. "Thank you," she said.

"For what?" Clifford asked.

"For just because," Emily Elizabeth told him.
"The parade was for Birdwell Island's birthday.
But it wouldn't be Birdwell Island without you."